One day, Debbie came
home from school and said,
"It's your birthday, Mog! And
we're going to have a party!"

"Mummy is baking a lovely cake," said Debbie.

MOG'S
Birthday

Judith Kerr

HarperCollins *Children's Books*

More Mog stories to treasure:

Mog the Forgetful Cat

Mog's Christmas

Mog and the Baby

Mog in the Dark

Mog's ABC

Mog and Bunny

Mog on Fox Night

Mog and the Granny

Mog and the V.E.T.

Mog's Bad Thing

Goodbye Mog

With special thanks to Lydia Barram and Ian Craig

First published in hardback in Great Britain by HarperCollins *Children's Books* in 2020

This paperback edition first published in 2021

10 9 8 7 6 5 4 3 2 1

ISBN: 978-0-00-846953-5

HarperCollins *Children's Books* is a division of HarperCollins*Publishers* Ltd,
1 London Bridge Street, London, SE1 9GF

www.harpercollins.co.uk

HarperCollins*Publishers*, 1st Floor, Watermarque Building, Ringsend Road, Dublin 4, Ireland

Text and illustrations copyright © Kerr-Kneale Productions Ltd 2020

Printed in China

"And there will be presents for you too."

"Oh no," thought Mog.
"I don't like birthday parties."

"There will be too many people in my house,
and too many strange things," thought Mog.

"There could even be a baby in my house.

I don't like babies. They break things."

"There will be too much
noise, and running about."

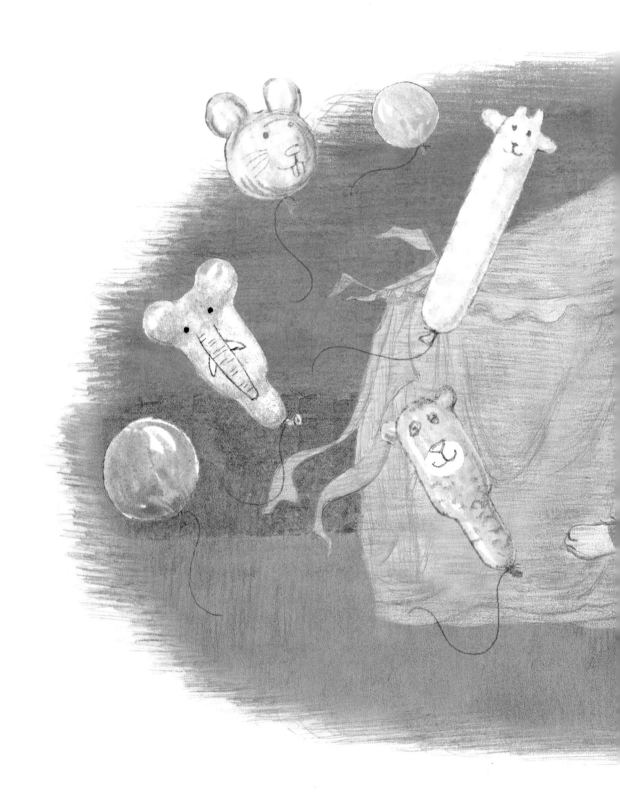

"There might even be

scary things at the party!"

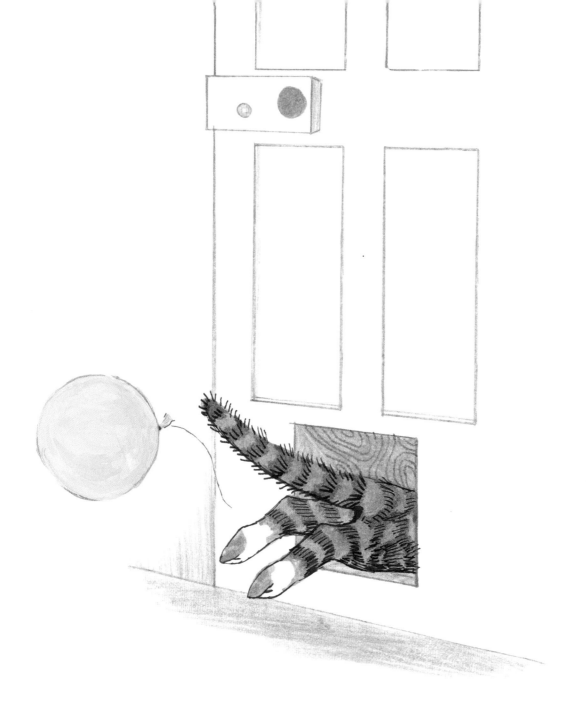

"Birthdays, and parties, are bad,"
thought Mog. "I'm getting out."

And she did. She ran outside
into the garden to hide.

Mog went to sleep in the tree, and had a lovely dream. It was a dream about a party with her family. And eggs.

Suddenly, Mog woke up
to a noise in the garden.
It was Debbie and Nicky.

They were sad because it was time
for Mog's birthday party, and they
couldn't find her anywhere.

"Poor Debbie and
Nicky," thought Mog.
"They'll never manage
a party without me."

And she jumped
straight out of
the tree.

"Oh, Mog! There you are!" said Debbie.

Mog went inside with Debbie and Nicky.

She saw that there were no strange people,
or babies, and there was a wonderful cake
just for Mog, and a new basket.

"Birthdays aren't so bad after all,
are they, Mog?" said Mr Thomas.

"No," thought Mog. "I suppose not."